the fly
and
the tree

JAMES I MORROW

The Book Guild Ltd

First published in Great Britain in 2020 by
The Book Guild Ltd
9 Priory Business Park
Wistow Road, Kibworth
Leicestershire, LE8 0RX
Freephone: 0800 999 2982
www.bookguild.co.uk
Email: info@bookguild.co.uk
Twitter: @bookguild

Typeset in 12pt Adobe Jenson Pro

Printed and bound in the UK by TJ International, Padstow, Cornwall

ISBN 978 1913208 578

British Library Cataloguing in Publication Data.

A catalogue record for this book is available from the British Library.

MIX
Paper from
responsible sources
FSC® C013056

For Suzanne
my editor-in-chief.
(Not only for this book but for my life in general.)

preface

Medical science is constantly moving forward, exploring new areas and pushing back the boundaries of the unknown or the unexplained.

Sometimes, though, the research itself may yield unexpected results. If so, as any good researcher knows, it is important to return to basics in order to re-challenge the source, the methodology and the conclusions reached, so as to account for, prove or refute any such anomalous result.

chapter one

September 2018

The young woman slipped softly out of the bed and began tiptoeing around its frame. Slowly and as quietly as she could manage, she edged her way across the floor, trying to make her escape from the darkened and unfamiliar room. Onward, towards where she hoped that she remembered the bedroom door was.

Reaching it, she felt around the wooden frame until she located the doorknob. The door creaked as it opened the first few inches.

Alarmed by the noise, she glanced around quickly. Through the gloom she could just perceive his form, still lying on his back on top of the bed, half in and half out of the covers. His chest was rising and falling rhythmically in time with his audible heavy breathing.

Satisfied that he was still deep in his post-coital slumber, she eased her way through the only partially opened door and on, out into the dark coolness of the landing.

The corridor was illuminated only by a thin filament of pale moonlight that was emitted from the small window at the head of the stairs. Despite the window being moist with condensation, she glimpsed the frost already starting to glisten on the bare branches of a shadowy tree beyond, now bereft of its leafy summer camouflage.

She pulled the door behind her but did not completely close it. She dared not risk any further noise, not now that she was so close to making good her escape. Each bare foot alighted softly in turn on each alternate carpeted stair. As she descended, Baz struggled into the towelling dressing robe that she had plucked from the back of the bedroom door. It was many sizes too big for her tiny frame. She pulled it tighter around herself, trembling a little as she did so. The robe acted as much a shield against her own internal fears as it did against the exterior coldness of the darkened house.

Finally reaching the bottom of the stairs, she gripped the banister and tried to regain her bearings. The kitchen was down the hall to her right. The sitting room, in which they had spent most of the evening listening to music and drinking wine, was directly in front of her. She felt suddenly a little lightheaded. Was the wine starting to go to her head or was it just the situation in which she found herself beginning to register? She steadied herself against the banister. Peering through the gloom to her left and at the end of a short narrow hallway, she could see the moonlight from the garden shimmering through the leaded windows that punctuated the external door of the neat Georgian cottage around which she stumbled.

She felt her way along the walls of the narrow corridor. She could touch the opposing walls simultaneously as she edged forward. Every so often a piece of furniture impeded her cautious progress; at first it was a mahogany table set against the wall, jutting out just far enough to allow her to stub her toe painfully against its wooden leg. She bit her lip, so as not to cry out with the sudden pain. Then it was a coat stand, heavy with discarded coats and jackets. She struggled past, trying not to dislodge any of the clothing, in case she were to leave any clue to her nocturnal expedition. Even the house itself seemed to be trying to entrap her.

When she reached her goal, it was not the outside door, but rather a smaller and less imposing interior-panelled door of distressed pine, which stood just to the left of its more formidable cousin. She felt for the handle and turned it. The door slid open silently on well-oiled and frequently used hinges. Swiftly, she stepped inside and closed the door silently behind her.

Standing for a moment, her back pressed hard against the closed door, she listened for sounds of movement within the house. All was still and quiet, except for the pounding of her heart within her chest and the short stabs of her quickened breathing. She stood upright and still for a few minutes longer, trying, in vain, to control the heady mixture of excitement and fear that seemed to suffuse her entire being.

Finally, recognising that complete control was beyond her, but that her volatile emotions were sufficiently suppressed to allow her to proceed, she surveyed the small room in which she now found herself. From the guided tour that he had insisted on earlier in the evening, she already knew that this room served as his study. He had ushered her briefly in and even more quickly out on the grounds of its level of untidiness and disorganisation. Among the small piles of half-read books and the larger piles of bills and letters, some even carefully replaced in their envelopes, she spotted the box files, all carefully and individually labelled.

The box files were on the shelves to the right and there should be a desk directly in front of her, she thought. Very little light penetrated the crack in the heavy curtains. She groped her way forward towards the desk, arms outstretched. Her knee struck its heavy wooden frame; her hands hovered three inches above its surface. 'Damn,' she whispered under her breath.

She fumbled around and across the desk's leather-covered surface. At last she found a small lamp perched on the corner of the desk and searched around it until she located the switch. The room filled with the incandescent glow from the energy saving light bulb. The young woman blinked her eyes adjusting to the sudden brightness and clarity of vision. Then, fully adapted once again, she moved over to examine the shelves upon which her target lay.

She examined each of the files in turn, finally removing the one that she had spotted earlier in the evening. The label had fixated itself into her consciousness despite the brusqueness of her earlier visit to this small inner sanctum. The label bore the name 'CATHY' in bold black ink. She examined it carefully; there were no other clues as to its contents.

The name 'Cathy' seemed somehow alien to Baz Clifford, a medical researcher who now posed as a sort of do-it-yourself detective. Baz had always thought of her as 'Catherine', Mrs Catherine Marsden; any earlier reference had always been in the longer, more formal format. Seeing her name written out before her in this more familiar form had taken her aback momentarily.

Regaining her composure, Baz cautiously lifted the lid of the box and peered nervously inside, as if half-expecting something to leap out, screeching and yelling and grappling at her throat. She could sense her heartbeat quicken again and her breath start to come in short pants as the adrenaline pumped once more around her body. Finally satisfied that the box contained no unpleasant or unexpected apparition, she allowed the lid to fall open and permitted herself to examine its contents in more detail. A few photographs, some official-looking papers and certificates, and a bundle of letters bound in a piece of faded red ribbon. Nothing more.

Suppressing her disappointment, Baz pulled out one of the photographs and studied it. It was just a typical family portrait. Of poor quality and indefinite age, it revealed a happy couple, each, Baz guessed, in their mid-twenties, smiling broadly towards the camera, the man's arm around his female companion's shoulders, her arm clasped tightly around his waist. The couple wore matching polo shirts and shorts; Baz winced slightly at the vision of apparent marital harmony suddenly confronting her. The couple stood under a large tree in dappled sunlight, their profiles set against a backdrop of a tall privet hedge and clear cloudless sky. The man was instantaneously recognisable as that of her bedfellow now soundly asleep upstairs. The woman, however, was not so familiar. Baz had read so much and in so much minute detail of 'Cathy', or 'Catherine', or whatever she cared to call herself, that she had built up a careful mental picture of her. The reality now before her was at odds with the mental picture she had nurtured. Baz knew that she was in her early thirties, five foot four inches tall, had dark brown hair, brown eyes, had no visible or other blemishes to speak of and was considered attractive by those who had known her. But this was Baz's first actual opportunity to see a photograph, albeit an old one, of the woman who had so engrossed and so dominated her thoughts over these last few difficult months.

The photograph was grainy, but the woman's features were remarkable nonetheless. Her face was angular, more distinguished, and her cheekbones a little more prominent than Baz had imagined, but nevertheless it was inescapable that the picture of 'Cathy' that Baz now held tightly in her hand was indeed that of Catherine Marsden. Baz removed more of the photographs and examined each in turn. Each

5

picture portrayed the same, often smiling, but occasionally more reserved, features of the young woman that Baz now recognised as Catherine Marsden.

Replacing the pile of photographs in the box file, taking care to retain their original order and position, she transferred her attention to the small bundle of letters. Some were still in their original envelopes and all were tightly secured by the faded red ribbon. Removing the bundle and laying it on the floor, Baz knelt down to examine it in more detail. It reminded her of her own teenage years: a bundle of private letters – love letters, perhaps – received or perhaps never sent, letters from an earlier age of innocence.

Even though the letters were written on a variety of different stationeries and from a number of different geographical areas, if the stamps and postmarks were anything to go by, they all appeared to be written in the same hand, as if from a single author. Baz selected a raggedly opened envelope and removed the folded sheet of paper contained therein. Baz's hand trembled slightly as she read on:

23/2/17

My dearest Cathy,

I cannot bear being separated from you. My whole being aches to be with you once again. I miss your beauty, your cleverness, your humour, the way you dismiss my concerns, your ability to rationalise and make the best of any situation, basically I miss everything that is you.

I am here in this lonely little office (as usual, duty calls). But even as I sit in this dismal little box of a room, just by sitting in front of this piece of paper and writing these few sad, pathetic words, I know that I am writing to you, the woman that I love, and this lifts my spirits.

I cannot yet take in our conversation at our last brief meeting. I know deep down that you want to be with me and I yearn to be with you.
So please reconsider, I hate being apart from you.
We need to work things out properly, make plans. Build a future together.

With deepest love,
Liam

Baz examined the rest of the letters. All had been written within the last couple of years and in all, the writer professed his undying love to Cathy. All appeared to express similar sentiments. As she read on, Baz felt a growing sense of guilt and shame. Guilt at the means she had employed to achieve this insight and shame at the intrusion this insight had revealed into former lives and former secrets that were not hers and to which she had no right.

A sudden noise startled her. She dropped the letters and glanced around. A few moments passed and nobody appeared. It had simply been the creaking of a wooden timber, the sort of noise that all older houses make as the temperature within rises or falls. She regathered the bundle of letters and tied them up with the piece of red ribbon. Then she pulled her robe tighter around her shoulders; she felt the cold even more acutely now.

Replacing everything within the box file, she returned it to the shelf in its original position. One last check ensured that she had not left any trace of her nocturnal adventure. Satisfied, she extinguished the light and made her way blindly back the way that she had come.

Entering the bedroom, she stood for a moment at the doorway and listened for his heavy breathing. Reassuring herself that he was still asleep, she edged her way around the bed and slipped once more back under the covers. She shivered, shaking off the cold of the house, allowing the warmth of the duvet to envelope her once more. Her partner rolled unconsciously towards her and a sleepy arm stretched across her abdomen. She pushed it away, but gently enough so as not to waken him. Lying on her back, she peered through the darkness at the outline of ceiling above. She knew that she wouldn't sleep now. That, which she had such high hopes might have produced some answers, had only given rise to more questions. The principal among which now were:

Who the hell was Liam?

And what part did he play in Cathy's death?

chapter two

Three Months Earlier...

'Fancy some lunch, Baz?'

Baz glanced up from the microscope lens. Squinting to refocus, she became aware of a set of gleaming white teeth and a fresh, smiling complexion, topped with a mop of golden hair. As she took in more of her visitor, she was a little disappointed to see a gangly frame dressed in an ill-fitting and slightly stained white laboratory coat.

'Oh, hi, Josh. Didn't hear you come in. What was that you said?'

'I was, um… just wondering if you wanted a bit of a break. Perhaps join me for a bite of lunch?' Baz noted that Joshua Hewitt, the lab technician, shifted from one foot to the other as he repeated his invitation. There had been a degree of confidence in his voice as he had addressed the back of her head, but now that Baz had turned around, any semblance of self-belief had drained from him.

Baz fixed Josh in her gaze. It amused her that he seemed to always fidget when she was around. She hadn't noticed him behave that way with any of the other students. With them he was always courteous and polite, never fidgety. Baz watched as he seemed to be struggling to suppress his nervousness, but that only served to make his awkwardness even more apparent. She hadn't always been aware of the effect that her physical features had on the male sex, but in recent years it had become more apparent. Usually she hid her attributes in a scruffy T-shirt and jeans, and tied her shoulder-length flecked chestnut hair back in a utilitarian pigtail. However, today, although she wore a white laboratory coat, it barely concealed the crisp cotton blouse and short skirt beneath. Today, she had allowed her hair to cascade freely. She guessed that it was her looks that made Josh nervous. Josh was, she thought, a little younger, or perhaps around her own age, twenty-six, but he seemed to lack her worldly confidence.

'Sorry, no time for lunch.'

'You take your work far too seriously, Baz. Everyone has time to take a break.' He motioned around at the other workbenches, now deserted.

'I know, I know, but I have my grant interview this afternoon, and if I don't get this stuff done now, the cells will degenerate and I'll have start all over again tomorrow. I'm sorry, Josh, I'd love to. Another time, perhaps?'

A slight bob of the head and a sheepish retreat suggested he thought she was being insincere, but in fact she had meant it. She liked Josh. He had proven helpful and attentive since her arrival at the Brightman Institute. She'd been fortunate in the first place to get a post there; it was, after all, one of the most respected research facilities in the south of England, though her first-class honours degree in biochemistry had undoubtedly helped. Josh had worked there longer than she had; in fact, she had heard that he'd got the job there as lab technician straight after leaving school and certainly he had proven invaluable to her as she had struggled to complete her PhD thesis. On any other day she would have joined him, but with the afternoon's grant renewal interview dominating her thoughts, she wouldn't be much company, not with that hanging over her head.

She swivelled back towards the microscope, staring at the intricate mosaic of cells before her. For once, though, she found her heart wasn't in the task. She began to feel increasingly guilty at her rejection of Josh's offer. He was, after all, only trying to be friendly. She looked up from her desk to spy him sitting alone in his office, quietly removing a tuna sandwich from its wrapping. She lifted herself down from the hard, wooden stool on which she had been perched since she had arrived at work earlier that morning. Pausing only to straighten her skirt, part of the suit she had chosen specifically for the forthcoming interview, she wound her way around the empty workbenches towards the office, pulling on her jacket as she did so.

Baz paused at the open door and then gently knocked at the frame. Josh had not detected her approach and he swung around, startled by the sudden intrusion, knocking over his bottle of cola in doing so.

'Oh, hi, Baz. Sorry, you startled me.' He wiped some errant crumbs from the corner of his mouth as he spoke, at the same time trying to retrieve the upturned bottle.

Leaning against the doorframe, Baz replied, 'Look, Josh, I'm really sorry about lunch, but I do have this interview and you know how important it is for me to secure the funding to allow me to complete my PhD.'

'Don't worry about it, as you said, another time, perhaps?'

'Well, that's just it.'

'What's just it?' There was a nervous hint to his voice, as if half-expecting another rebuttal.

'Well, I was just thinking—'

'Thinking, that's good. I was just reading…' he started to mumble, 'that the brain's a muscle, it needs to be exercised or it will degenerate. If you don't use it, you'll lose it, isn't that what they say?'

'Very good, but as I was saying,' continued Baz, undeterred, 'I was just thinking…'

Josh shifted nervously in his seat.

'…that once I've got this interview over, I'll probably feel like going out for a drink, but at the moment I've no-one to go out with and I was just wondering if you'd like to…?'

'You bet ya, I do.' Josh jumped to his feet excitedly.

'Great,' replied Baz, a little taken aback by his sudden surge of enthusiasm. 'See you in The George about 5.30.'

The next couple of hours were taken up with revising her presentation to the grant committee. Baz, being the person she was, did not wish to leave anything to chance. Although she had repeatedly been reassured by others that her work was of sufficient merit that she would breeze through any assessment of it, she was acutely aware of the importance of securing sufficient funding to allow her to complete the current project. So it was that come the appointed hour, she nervously fiddled with the hem of her skirt as she sat and waited patiently outside the interview room.

The door opened into the waiting area where Baz sat, catching her unawares, despite her heightened level of anxiety. The candidate whose appointment had been scheduled before hers emerged from the room beyond. Baz could not help but notice the ashen look on his face. Baz hoped that her own features did not portray a similar degree of anxiety. The door had closed again. *A few minutes' deliberation*, thought Baz, *and then it will be my turn.* She gripped the hem of her skirt even more tightly.

'Miss Clifford,' the voice announced from just inside the opening door. Baz leapt to her feet.

She paused, took a couple of deep breathes to steady herself and then she stepped into the room. Dimly lit and panelled in dark and musty wood, the room smelt of academia. The afternoon sunlight shone in dusty streams through the heavy leaded windows behind the three occupants of a large mahogany table. The rays of light seemed to Baz to focus themselves on the solitary empty chair on her side of the table as if a spotlight was shining on the seat reserved for the condemned criminal.

The middle-aged woman who had opened the door and bade Baz entry now closed it behind her and indicated to Baz to take her seat in the sunny spotlight, before she herself sat down in a chair beside the door and proceeded to take silent notes.

Guarding the entrance, thought Baz. *The bitch has the exit covered, no escape now.*

'You are very welcome, Miss… eh… Clifford, isn't it?'

The speaker was a distinguished-looking gentleman in, Baz estimated, his early sixties. He was seated in the centre of the three and appeared to be the chairman of the panel. He had spoken the words whilst consulting a large pile of documents on the table in front of him. He hadn't even bothered to look up from his papers as he had greeted her, Baz noted.

'Baz.'

The chairman, somewhat confused by the response, looked up. 'I'm sorry, what was that you said?'

'Baz.'

Now fearing that he was being in some way slighted, but worse, not understanding the insult.'What?' he said tetchily.

'Baz, short for Barbara, it's my name, Professor Blackwell-Jones.'

'Oh,' he replied.

From the corner of her eye, Baz could see Dr Morton, who sat at the left-hand end of the table, shoot her a warning glance, as if to tell her to behave. Dr Morton was Baz's immediate boss and knew only too well her feisty nature. That glance was simply to tell her that this was neither the time nor the place to promote her independence.

Quickly recovering the former composure, for which he was certain, at least in his own mind, that he was famed, the eminent professor continued, 'We prefer a little formality on these occasions, I think you'll find, Miss Clifford.'

'Quite so,' rejoined the final panellist, a woman in her mid-fifties.

'I am sure we are all familiar to you Miss Clifford, so I won't waste time on introductions.'

It was true that Baz knew Dr Morton, having worked in his department over the preceding months; Professor Blackwell-Jones she did not know but knew to see. He was the Professor of Medicine at the hospital and university and was therefore at every panel, committee, scientific or strategy meeting that was going. Baz was also well aware of his importance and had accepted Dr Morton's warning shot with a look of suitable humility. The third person, the solitary woman on the panel, was not, however, immediately recognisable to Baz. *The single most striking thing about this woman*, thought Baz, *is her undoubted plainness*. There was just no other way to put it. Plain she was, there was just nothing attractive, nor indeed anything outstandingly unattractive, about her. Her face, which bore